Little Bear's
Magical Christmas

igloobooks

One Christmas, Little Bear said, "I'm not writing to Santa this year.
There's no point sending a letter, because Santa won't be here."

"Why won't Santa come?" asked his curious mum and dad.
"Well you see," said Little Bear, "I've been a little bit bad."

"I went to the kitchen cupboard and dipped my paw in the honey. Oh, but it was so delicious, so **dribbly** and **sticky** and **runny**."

"Then I didn't tidy my room when Mummy told me to."

"Don't worry about that," said Mummy Bear.
"I'm not cross with you."

"Oh, but there's more,"
said Little Bear.
"Quite a bit more than that."

"When Aunty came to stay,
I tried on her **fancy** new hat."

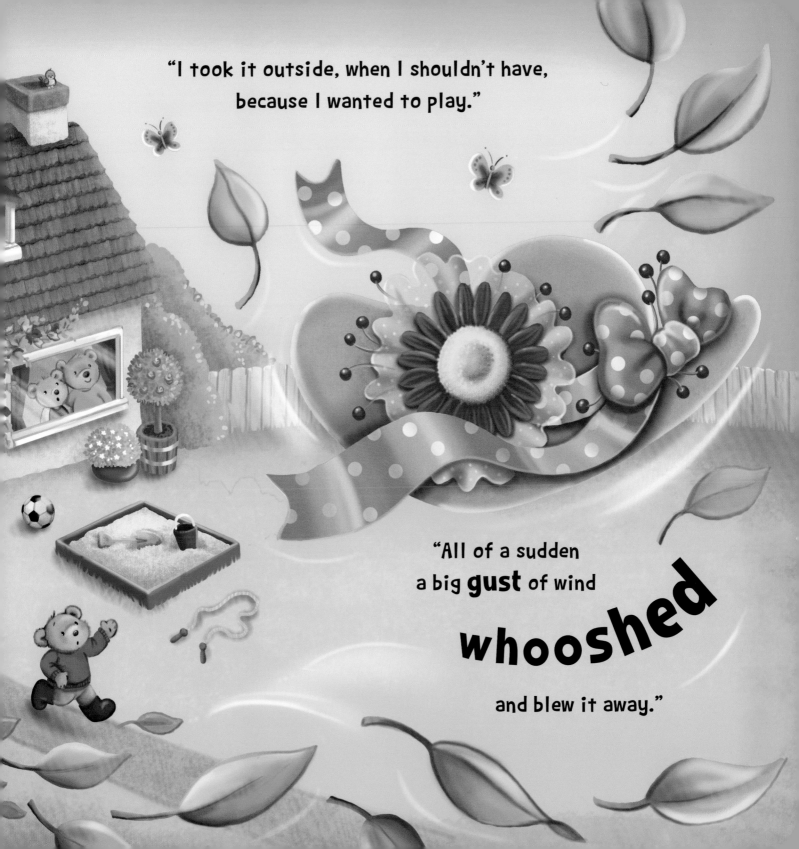

"I took it outside, when I shouldn't have, because I wanted to play."

"All of a sudden
a big **gust** of wind

whooshed

and blew it away."

Little Bear told his mum and dad about when he'd made too much noise.

And when his friends came over, he had refused to share his toys.

"So, you see," said Little Bear, "why I can't write to Santa Claus."
He looked sadly at the Christmas tree and **twiddled** his furry paws.

"Oh, Bear," said Daddy kindly, "you're forgetting the good things you've done."

"Like when you made Aunty giggle, and she had lots of fun."

"And remember when you gave your friends your tin of **yummy** treats? You shared them out at the picnic, so everyone had some sweets."

"Santa won't think you're bad," said Mummy, "because you made mistakes. He'll remember **special** times like when you made Daddy cupcakes."

Suddenly Little Bear's happiness all came **flooding** back.
"Go and write Santa that letter," said Mummy, "and I'll make you a snack."

So Little Bear wrote a letter and posted it that day.
An elf took it to Santa, at the North Pole far away.

"I wonder if Santa got my letter," said Little Bear on Christmas Eve.
"Magic things happen at Christmas," said Mummy. "You just need to believe."

Little Bear tried to stay awake, but soon slept quiet as a mouse.
It was then that Santa and his reindeer **flew** right over his house.

With a **jingle** of bells, Santa left presents under the Christmas tree.
He wrote a special note for Little Bear to see.

"Ho, ho, ho," said Santa, as he flew off into the air.
"There'll be smiles tomorrow morning for one happy little bear."

On Christmas morning Little Bear **bounded** out of bed.

Under the tree were presents.
"Santa's been," he said.

Santa's note said,

"Dear Little Bear,
I've left you some presents here.
Thank you for being so good.
I'll see you again next year."